LONGMAN CLASSICS

The Snow Goose

and other stories

Paul Gallico

Simplified by Christine Rose

Longman

Longman Group UK Limited,
Longman House, Burnt Mill, Harlow,
Essex CM20 2JE, England
and Associated Companies throughout the world.

First published 1987

ISBN 0-582-54141-7

Set in 10/13 point Linotron 202 Versailles
Produced by Longman Group (FE) Limited
Printed in Hong Kong

Acknowledgements

'Photographs © BBC' 1971.

The cover background is a wallpaper design called NUAGE,
courtesy of Osborne and Little plc.

Stage 1: 1300 word vocabulary

Please look under *New words* at the back of this book
for explanations of words outside this stage.

Introduction

Paul Gallico

The very popular American writer Paul Gallico was born in New York in 1897. He is best known for his novels and short stories, though he wrote a great deal on sports and other subjects. Some of his stories, like *The Snow Goose* and *The Poseidon Adventure*, have been made into films. In other cases he wrote the film or television play first, and the book followed. He died in 1976.

Gallico travelled very widely, and he spent a lot of time in Britain. Many of his stories, like *The Snow Goose* (1941), have a British setting. Among these are the four very amusing "Mrs 'Arris" novels, beginning with *Mrs 'Arris goes to Paris* (1958). In that story, Mrs Harris, the lovable London cleaning woman, goes completely out of her "class", and brings understanding and happiness to people in the fashion world about which she had only dreamed. (Like Private Potton in *The Snow Goose*, Mrs Harris "drops" her *h* sounds, even in saying her own name.)

A lot of Paul Gallico's fiction is sentimental, meaning that it calls up our tender feelings, inviting our tears at the end of *The Snow Goose* and our joy at Mrs Harris's happy moments. In fact, the three stories in this book may be described as "novelettes" because of their sentimental nature, and because they are longer than most "short stories" but shorter than a full-length "novel". There is a collection of Paul Gallico's short stories in the Longman Structural Readers series (Stage 3): *Love is a Gimmick*. The stories are set in America, Italy, France and Greece.

The Stories

These notes on two of the stories in this book will help your understanding and enjoyment of them.

The Snow Goose: The wild goose called the snow goose lives in Canada and flies south in winter in the way Philip Rhayader describes in *The Snow Goose*. Its feathers are pure white except for the tips – the very ends – of the wings, which are black. It flies very strongly. We don't know whether a snow goose would follow a man – even as kind a man as Philip – in the way Princess the snow goose does in the story.

The hero of *The Snow Goose* takes part in the rescue at Dunkirk (Dunkerque) in France in World War II. His part is, of course, fiction. But a very large number of people like Philip did answer the call for small boats to take men off the beaches, and many of them were killed or hurt.

In a well prepared sudden drive across south-eastern Belgium, the German army cut off the whole of the British army in Europe and some French and Belgian forces. A part of the French force fought a fierce battle to stop the German advance while the most surprising collection of boats took about 338,000 British, French and Belgian soldiers off the beaches between 26 May and 14 June 1940. The *Kentish Maid* did take part. She was an old holiday pleasure boat with steam engines driving paddle-wheels at the sides. You can still see her in the collection of famous old ships at the St Katharine Dock, near Tower Bridge in London.

The Silver Swans: Paul Gallico lived for a time in the part of London that he describes in *The Silver Swans.* Chelsea, especially Cheyne Walk by the River Thames, is a part that has attracted a lot of writers, artists and people like the imaginary Doctor Horatio Fundoby.

The swans on the River Thames are not now as dirty as the ones that came past the houseboat in the story. The river has been cleaned up. A sailing ship like the *Poseidon* can reach that part of the river, but her masts have to be lowered to allow her to pass under thirteen bridges.

Starting with Charles Darwin (*On the Origin of Species,* 1859), the Galapagos Islands have been of interest to very many scientists, like Richard Hadley in this story, because of the unusual animals, birds, fishes and plants to be found there. The islands lie in the Pacific Ocean, about 965 kilometres from the coast of South America.

The Snow Goose

In the spring of 1930 a man bought an old, empty light-house. It stood at the mouth of a river and was in the middle of marshland. This place was called the Great Marsh. It was a wild and lonely place where no one lived and the only sounds were made by the many birds that made their homes there.

The man's name was Philip Rhayader and he was a painter. He painted pictures of the birds and the marsh-land. Philip lived at the lighthouse because he wanted to live alone. Every two weeks he went to the village of Chelmbury for the supplies he needed. When the villagers first saw him they stared, because Philip was a hunchback. His left arm was thin and twisted, and his left hand was bent like a bird's foot. His appearance made the villagers afraid of him. But as time passed they grew used to his strange ways.

Philip was twenty-seven when he came to the lighthouse. He had lived in many places before coming there. He had tried hard to make friends with the people he met. But other men did not want to be friends with Philip. The sight of his twisted body turned them against him. Women he might have loved turned their eyes away when they saw him. So they never found out that he was a gentle, loving man who loved all things that lived. But he did not hate these people; his heart was so full of love. He could only feel sadness for them.

1

Instead he turned to his birds and his paintings. He owned a sailing boat which he could sail very well. Often, when it was very windy, he used his teeth to hold the ropes, instead of his weak left arm. He sailed up and down the rivers, and sometimes out to sea. Often he was gone for many days. He went looking for different birds to draw and photograph. He also caught some birds in a net. He put them in the enclosure he had built at the side of the lighthouse. He never shot at a bird and anyone who did shoot at them was told not to come near the lighthouse. He was a friend to all living things and so all living things trusted him and became his friends.

One afternoon a girl came to the door. It was November and Philip had been at the lighthouse for three years. She was twelve years old, thin and untidy. She had fair hair and blue eyes. The thought of knocking at the door filled her with fear. She had heard strange stories about the man who lived in the lighthouse. But the reason she had come was more important than her fear: in one of the stories about him, the villagers had said that this hunchback could make wounded or sick birds better.

She knocked at the door. Slowly it opened. When she saw Philip, she nearly ran away. But when he spoke he had a kind voice.

"What do you want, little girl?" he asked gently.

She pushed out her arms, which held a large, white bird. There was blood on its feathers and on the front of her dress. She gave the bird to him.

"I found it," she said, so quietly that he could hardly hear her. "It's hurt. Is it still alive?"

"Yes. Yes, I think so," he said, looking at it. "Come in, child, come in."

Philip with the snow goose in his arms

The girl still felt afraid but she went in, because she wanted to see inside the lighthouse.

Philip put the bird on the table. The room was warm and there was a coal fire burning. The bird moved and Philip turned to the girl.

"Where did you find it?" he asked.

"In the marsh, where the wild-fowlers have been," she said. "What kind of bird is it?"

"It's a snow goose from Canada," he told her. Then he said to himself, in surprise: "I wonder how it came here?"

"Can you make it better?"

"Yes, yes. We'll try," he replied.

Philip put the things he needed on the table. As his gentle hands began to work on the bird, the child watched with wide-open eyes.

"She has been shot, poor thing," he said, "and one of her legs is broken. We must cover the part of the wing that is hurt. Then, in the spring, the feathers will grow and she will be able to fly again."

As he worked, he told her a wonderful story.

"She's only a young snow goose, you know – about a year old. She comes from Canada. That's a big country far, far away across the ocean. In Canada the winters are very, very cold. So each year the snow geese fly south to warmer countries. But this time, as this snow goose was flying south, she was caught in a great storm. It was a wild, wild storm. The wind picked her up and carried her with it for many days and nights. She had strong wings, but they were not strong enough to help her. At last the storm ended and she was able to fly south again. But now she was flying over England. She was lost and tired, so she landed here. When she came down to rest we ought to

4

have received her like a visiting princess. Instead of that, a wild-fowler tried to shoot her."

He put a thin piece of wood on the broken leg to hold it straight. As he was mending the bird's leg, he told her about the birds in his enclosure.

"The geese in the enclosure have flown all the way from Iceland and Spitzbergen," he told her. "They arrive in October. There are so many of them that they make the sky look dark. The sound of their wings is like a strong wind."

He finished mending the leg. They went outside and put the snow goose with the other birds. As he placed her gently in the enclosure he said, "In a few days she will be much better. Let's call her the Lost Princess."

The girl looked pleased. Then she noticed that some of the birds were unable to fly.

"What is the matter with those birds?" she asked, pointing at two birds who were trying to fly.

"I have clipped the ends of their wings," he said, "so that they can't fly and have to stay here."

"Does it hurt them?" she asked.

"No, no, little girl," he said, laughing gently. "The feathers will grow again next spring."

"Why do you clip their wings, then?"

"So that these birds will show the others who come," he said, "that here there is food and a safe place to stay. In the spring they will fly back to their homes in the north."

All the time that she had been watching him work and listening to him speak, she had forgotten the stories about him. Suddenly she remembered. Without saying another word she ran to the path that led to the village.

Philip called after her. "What's your name?"

She stopped running and turned to answer him.

"It's Fritha," she called back.

"Where do you live?" he asked.

"With the fishing people in the village," she replied.

"Will you come back in a day or two to see how the Princess is?"

She did not answer at once, but at last he heard her answer: "Yes."

Then she ran along the path, her hair blowing out behind her.

The snow goose got better very quickly. By the middle of winter she was able to limp about in the enclosure with the other birds. Fritha often walked to the lighthouse to see the Princess, because with each visit her fear of Philip became less and less. She loved the story that Philip told her about this strange, white princess. He showed her a map of where the goose had come from.

Then, one morning in June, the Princess left them. Fritha was at the lighthouse at the time. She saw her flying into the sky.

"Look. Look at the Princess! Is she leaving us?" she shouted to Philip.

He came running from where he had been painting. He was just in time to see the snow goose disappear into the distance.

"Yes, the Princess is going home," he said quietly. "Listen, she is saying goodbye."

As they stood listening, there came through the air the sad call of the snow goose.

Fritha did not come to the lighthouse after the snow goose had gone. Philip was once again alone with his birds and his paintings.

Then, one day, a wonderful thing happened in Philip's

Philip spends his time painting pictures

life. It was October again and he was in the enclosure, feeding the birds. There was a cold northeast wind blowing which, with the noise from the sea, made it hard to hear any other sounds. Suddenly Philip heard the high, clear call of a bird. He turned his head and looked into the sky. At first he could only see a small dot. Then as the dot came closer it grew into the shape of a bird. As Philip watched, the bird flew round the lighthouse and dropped into the enclosure. What he saw made his eyes fill with tears. It was the snow goose! She walked round the enclosure as if she had never been away. Philip knew that she could not have been home to Canada.

"I suppose she spent the summer in Greenland," he said to himself. Then when the time came to fly south again, she had remembered Philip's kindness and had returned.

At once Philip thought of Fritha. He knew that she must be told. So when he went to the village for supplies, he left a note at the post office. It said:

> *Tell Fritha, who lives with the*
> *fishing people, that the Princess*
> *is back.*

Three days later Fritha came to the lighthouse. She was taller but still untidy.

The years passed by. On the Great Marsh hardly anything changed. The sea continued to flow in and out and the birds came and went with the seasons. For Philip the passing of time was shown by the coming and going of the snow goose. When the snow goose was at the lighthouse, Fritha visited Philip. She sailed with him in his boat and they caught birds to put in the enclosure. Fritha learned many things from Philip. He taught her everything about the wild birds. Sometimes she cooked for him and she also learned how to get his paints ready.

But when the snow goose left in the summer, Fritha did not come to the lighthouse. For some reason she did not feel that she could visit Philip when the bird was not there.

Then, one year, the Princess did not return. Philip thought that his heart would break. He was lonely once more. He spent all of his time painting. He painted all winter and the next summer. He did not see Fritha at all. But in October he heard again the cry of the snow goose. She had come back. Philip was so happy that he went into the village at once. As before, he left a note at the post office for Fritha.

This time it was a month before she came to the lighthouse. When he saw her, he was surprised to see that she had grown up. She was not a child any more.

From now on, the snow goose stayed at the lighthouse for longer and longer each year. She followed Philip about and sometimes went into the lighthouse after him. And so time went on ...

One spring something happened in the world outside the Great Marsh. It changed the lives of Philip, Fritha and the snow goose: the Second World War began. It was 1940, and the birds had left early for their summer homes in the north lands. As Philip and Fritha stood and watched them go, the snow goose started to fly away too. But she did not fly with the others. Instead, she just flew around their heads a few times and landed back in the enclosure.

"She isn't going!" said Fritha, surprised. "The Princess is staying."

"Yes," said Philip in a weak voice, because he too was

surprised. "She'll stay," he said. "She'll never fly away again. The Lost Princess is not lost now. This is her home and she has decided to stay."

As he said these words, Philip thought: "Fritha is like the snow goose. She, too, has come and gone from the lighthouse." Philip was used to Fritha's visits and he was happy when she came to see him and the snow goose.

She was a young woman now. As he turned and looked at her, he knew that he loved her. But he also knew that he could not tell her about his love. He did not frighten her at all now, but he felt that his appearance was unpleasant to her. So the words he wanted to say were locked in his heart. But the love he felt showed in his eyes.

Fritha turned to look at Philip as he finished speaking. She saw that he was lonely, but she also saw something she could not understand. It was a gentle, sad look that made her feel unhappy inside. She did not know what to say, and so she looked away.

For several minutes neither of them spoke. At last she said, "I ... I must go. I'm glad the Princess is staying. Now you'll not be so lonely. Goodbye."

As she walked quickly away, she heard him say sadly, "Goodbye, Fritha."

After a few minutes she stopped walking and turned to look back at the lighthouse. He was standing where she had left him. Then she turned towards the village and walked home, thoughtfully.

Fritha did not return to the lighthouse for three weeks. By then it was the end of May. It was early evening when she came. She saw the yellow light of Philip's lamp shining from where he kept his boat. She hurried down to the river's edge. The boat was moving gently from side to side.

10

Philip plans to sail in his boat to Dunkirk

Philip was putting drinking water, food, clothes and another sail into the boat. He heard her footsteps and turned round. He looked rather pale but also excited. She completely forgot about the snow goose.

"Philip! Are you going away?" she asked.

As he spoke she saw a look of excitement come into his eyes. It was the look of someone who has an important job to do.

"Fritha! I'm pleased you've come," he said. "Yes, I must go away. It won't be for long and I'll come back as soon as I can."

"Where must you go?" she asked.

Then his words poured out. He told her about Dunkirk, which was a seaside town across the Channel. On the beaches by Dunkirk there were British soldiers. They could not move because the sea was in front of them and the German army was behind them. Dunkirk was on fire and they had no hope of being saved. On the radio the government in London had asked everyone who owned a boat to cross the Channel. It wanted them to bring back as many soldiers as possible from the beaches.

"I heard about this when I was in the village getting supplies," he continued. "I'll cross the Channel in my boat, Fritha. I can take six men, perhaps seven, each time I sail from the beach to the large ships. The large ships have to wait in deep water – they can't go in any closer. Do you understand, now, why I have to go?"

Fritha did not understand about war or about what was happening to the soldiers on the beaches. She only knew that this journey was dangerous for Philip.

"Philip, must you go? You won't come back!" she cried. "Why do you have to go?"

With a gentle voice he told her why he had to go. "The

soldiers are like the birds we have cared for," he said. "Many of them are wounded, like the Lost Princess you found and brought to me. They are afraid of what will happen to them. They need my help, my dear, as the birds have done."

With a happy look in his eyes he continued, "At last I can do something to help in this war."

Fritha stared at him. He looked different. He did not seem ugly to her any more and she wanted to tell him this. But she did not know how to. She remembered the look she had seen in his eyes a few weeks ago. Now she knew what it was. It was love.

Suddenly she cried, "I'll go with you!"

He shook his head. "If you come, you'll take a soldier's place in the boat. I must go alone."

He put on his coat, climbed into the boat and set off. "Goodbye, Fritha," he called. "Look after the birds while I'm gone." As he sailed away, he turned and waved to her. She waved back, but she was too unhappy to wave properly.

"I'll take care of them, Philip," she replied, "and God take care of you."

It was night now. In the moonlight she watched the boat sail out to sea. Suddenly there was a sound of beating wings in the darkness behind her. As she looked up she could see the snow goose flying into the night sky. It went round the lighthouse once and then it flew out to sea – after the little boat.

"Take care of him, Princess," she called.

At last they were both out of sight. She turned and walked slowly back to the lighthouse.

The rest of the story about Philip and the snow goose is in

two parts. One of these parts is told by a soldier. The soldier – Private Potton – had just come back from Dunkirk. He was among the first two hundred soldiers to arrive home in England.

As the soldiers left the boat that had brought them across the Channel, they were met by several reporters. The reporters were from *The Times*, the *Evening News*, the *Daily Sketch* and the *Daily Express*. They had been sent from London to find out what had happened at Dunkirk. But many of the soldiers were wounded, or they were too tired to stop and talk. Private Potton was different. He was happy to tell anyone who would listen how he and his friend had been saved.

As he began to tell his story, the reporters wrote down what he said. Suddenly the man from the *Evening News* asked: "How do you mean ... 'it was hopeless'?"

Potton turned to answer him. "'Ow do I mean it was 'opeless? Well, there we were, on that beach, with no place to go to. The German army was behind us and the sea was in front of us. That's right, isn't it, Jock? 'E was there, too, Jock was.

"The bullets were coming at us from all sides ... from the air, too, as the planes dived low over the beaches. We all lay on that beach with our 'ands over our 'eads. The noise was so loud you couldn't 'ear yourself speak, could you, Jock?

"There was smoke everywhere. It was so thick at times you could almost taste it. We were coughing ... and out at sea we could 'ear the battle between the German planes and the British warships.

"We thought that any minute we'd be 'it by those bullets flying about. We were so tired and sick, we didn't know what to do. And 'alf a mile out at sea, there was the

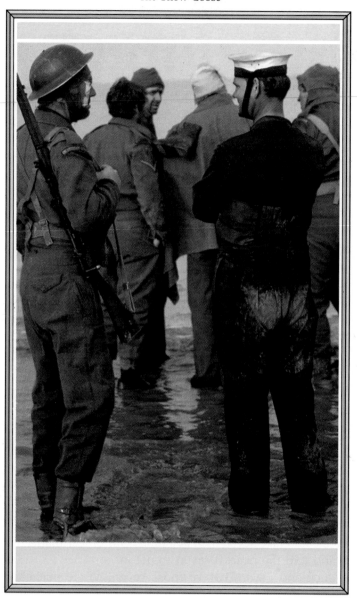

Soldiers on the beach at Dunkirk

Kentish Maid – this boat behind us. She used to sail out from Margate in the summer – I've been on 'er myself. Well, there she was waiting to take us 'ome – but we couldn't swim out to 'er and she couldn't come in any closer.

"Then, suddenly through the smoke, came this goose. A goose it was! I couldn't believe my eyes but Jock 'ere saw it too, didn't you, Jock? It was white and it went round and round over our 'eads.

"When Jock saw it, 'e shouted out that it meant death for all of us. But I shouted back that it meant good luck.

"Then through the smoke 'e comes – sailing in this little boat."

"Who comes?" asked the man from *The Times*.

"'Im. 'Im who saved us! 'E came sailing near to the beach, taking no notice of the guns and bombs. I've never been so pleased to see someone. If that 'ad been me I'd 'ave been too frightened to come anywhere near the beach – but not 'im. 'E sailed as if 'e was out sailing on a Sunday afternoon!

"But 'e was a strange-looking man, wasn't 'e, Jock? 'E 'ad a beard, a bent left 'and and an 'unched back. 'E 'ad a rope between 'is teeth and 'e was guiding the boat with 'is good 'and.

"Jock, 'ere, thought 'e was the Devil, didn't you, Jock? But I said 'e looked more like the pictures I'd seen of Jesus when I was in Sunday school.

"'E waved us out to 'is boat and shouted to our officer that 'e could take seven men at a time. Our officer thanked 'im and told the nearest seven to get in.

"Jock and I were two of those seven, so we pushed through the water to the boat. But it was 'ard work, going that short way, wasn't it, Jock? When we reached it we

16

were so tired we couldn't climb over the side. But 'e was strong, 'e was, and 'e pulled us in one by one.

"'E told us to lie in the bottom of the boat and then we were off. When I looked at the sail I was surprised the boat moved at all. It 'ad so many 'oles in it from the bullets – it looked like a net!

"And up there, over our 'eads, that goose flew round and round and round. Never stopped, did it, Jock?

"'There, I told you that goose meant good luck,' I said to Jock. When 'e 'ears me, at the back of the boat, 'e looks up and smiles at 'er – as if 'e 'ad known 'er all 'is life.

"When we got to the *Kentish Maid* we climbed up on to it. Then 'e and the goose went back to the beach for seven more soldiers.

"'E made journeys all afternoon and all night, too. 'E could see at night because Dunkirk was on fire: it lit up the sky! I don't know 'ow many journeys 'e made. 'E must 'ave been tired out – but 'e kept on going, didn't 'e, Jock?

"There was also a motorboat from the Thames Yacht Club and a big boat from Poole. Between them they saved all of us from that beach.

"'E was still there when we left. 'E waved goodbye to us and then sailed off towards Dunkirk – that goose with 'im.

"Ooh – it was strange to see that big goose flying round and round 'is boat as it sailed along.

"And 'ere we are in England. We don't know who 'e was or what 'appened to 'im, but 'e was a good man, 'e was. 'E saved our lives, didn't 'e, Jock?"

Another man who was at Dunkirk, helping to save the soldiers, was Commander Keith Emerson. He was sixty-seven years old then, but a few years before he

Philip saves the soldiers at Dunkirk

had been in the Royal Navy.

At four o'clock one morning, Commander Emerson was woken up by the telephone. He was asked to take a boat across the Channel to Dunkirk. The slow, but powerful boat pulled four big Thames river boats behind it. With these boats he crossed the Channel many times to save the soldiers on the beaches.

He was talking about it to another Royal Navy officer who had been at Dunkirk.

"Did you hear that strange story about a wild goose?" his friend asked. "Some of the men I brought back were talking about it. They said it appeared between Dunkirk and La Panne – and, if you saw it, you'd be saved."

"Hmm," said the commander, "a wild goose, you say? Well, I saw a white goose – and it was lucky for us, too. I'll tell you about it.

"We were on our way back from Dunkirk. At about six o'clock we saw a small sailing boat – and this white goose was standing on one of the sides. I decided to change the way we were going so as to have a look. As we drew nearer, I saw that there was a man lying in the bottom of the boat – a man with a beard. He was dead, poor man – he'd been shot many times.

"When we were beside the boat one of my men tried to put his hand on the side – but the goose beat her wings at him. He just couldn't get near.

"Suddenly someone gave a loud shout and pointed to something in the water. It was a mine! It was lucky for us that we'd gone to look at that boat. If we'd gone straight on, we would have hit it – and I certainly wouldn't be standing here now.

"We let the mine get past the last of our boats and then our men shot at it. There was a very loud explosion. When we looked for the sailing boat, it was gone. It must have gone down when the mine exploded. I'm afraid that the man went with his boat – he must have been tied to it. The goose rose in the air and flew round in circles where the boat had been. She flew round three times, as if she was saying goodbye. Then she flew off to the west. It was all very strange and rather sad," said the commander, as he finished his story.

After Philip had gone to France, Fritha stayed at the lighthouse on the Great Marsh taking care of the birds that could not fly away. She was waiting for something – but she didn't know what. During the first days after Philip left, she kept going to the sea wall to watch for his boat returning. But the days passed and Philip did not return. She spent some days looking in the storerooms of the lighthouse. In one of them she found Philip's paintings. Among them there was a picture of the day she had brought the snow goose to the lighthouse. It showed her standing at the door holding the snow goose in her arms. She thought it was strange that this was the only painting of the snow goose: the lost, wild bird that had made her and Philip friends.

It was the snow goose which let her know for certain that Philip would not return.

One evening, as she was standing by the lighthouse, she heard the call of the snow goose. She ran to the sea wall and looked up into the sky. When she saw the snow goose she looked down the river towards the sea. But she already knew that it was hopeless looking: there was no little sailing boat. The snow goose was alone. At that moment Fritha knew that she loved Philip and that she

Fritha knows Philip will never return

would never see him again. Tears filled her eyes. As she watched the snow goose she thought she could hear Philip's voice calling to her: "Fritha, Fritha, my love. Goodbye, my love."

"I love you, Philip," Fritha said aloud to herself.

For a minute Fritha thought that the snow goose was going to land in the enclosure. But, after coming down very low, she flew up again into the sky. She circled the lighthouse once and then climbed higher into the sky. As Fritha watched the snow goose, she did not see it as a bird. She saw it as the soul of Philip coming to say goodbye before disappearing for ever.

She stretched out her arms up into the sky, crying: "Goodbye, Philip. Goodbye."

She stopped crying and watched in silence long after the snow goose had gone. Then she went into the lighthouse and found the picture that Philip had painted of her and the snow goose. She held it to her chest and walked home slowly along the old sea wall.

Each night for the next few weeks, Fritha went to the lighthouse and fed the birds that could not fly. Then, early one morning, a German aeroplane flew over the lighthouse. The pilot mistook it for a place that had to be bombed. The plane flew high into the sky and then dived towards the lighthouse. As the bombs landed on it there were several loud explosions: the lighthouse was gone.

As usual, Fritha came in the evening to feed the birds. She was walking along the path when she suddenly stopped. She couldn't believe her eyes. The lighthouse and the enclosure had disappeared. There was nothing left of them. There was only the sea covering the place where the lighthouse had once stood.

The Enchanted Doll

The story I am going to tell you began three years ago –
and it all happened because of a doll.

I am a doctor and my name is Stephen Amony. The
house where I live and work is in London, by the River
Thames.

I can clearly remember that October day three years
ago. From my window I could see the early morning sun
shining on the river.

I left my house to go and buy a copy of *The Times*,
which I did each morning. There was a flower shop on the
corner of the road where I lived. As I reached the corner
I could see the brightly-coloured flowers. I turned into
Abbey Lane.

A few minutes later I arrived at the shop to buy my
Times. Before I went inside I stopped to look in the
window. I had suddenly remembered that it was my
niece's birthday next week.

As usual it was full of toys, games, sweets, paper and
pens. Some of them looked as if they had been there for
years. I had almost decided that there was nothing my
niece would like when I saw a doll. She was almost hidden
in the corner of the window. She was made of cloth, but it
was her face that I noticed. Although the face was painted,
it had a lovely, gentle look. But the eyes seemed rather sad
and I felt sorry for her sitting in that crowded window. I
decided to have a closer look at her.

The shop was owned by a man named Jim Carter. As I

walked in, he said brightly, "Good morning, Doctor Amony! Do you want a copy of *The Times* as usual?"

"Yes, please, Jim," I replied. "I also need a present for my niece. I'd like to see that doll in your window – the one in the corner, made of cloth."

Jim looked surprised and said, "That doll? Well, she's rather unusual but she's also very expensive, Doctor."

He took her from the window and gave her to me. When I took the doll from him I nearly dropped her in surprise. She was made so beautifully that she seemed almost lifelike. Her clothes had been made by hand, and the face, which I could now see clearly, was hand-painted by an artist. It was lovely. Whoever had made her had done so with much love and care. It was this love that I thought I could sense in her face.

I put her down gently. "How much do you want for her, Jim?" I asked.

"Twelve pounds," he replied.

I must have looked surprised because Jim said, "I said she was expensive, didn't I? But I'll sell her to you for eleven pounds. In the centre of London they cost as much as twenty pounds."

"Who makes them?" I asked. I was curious to know about the person who made such lovely dolls.

"The woman lives in Hardley Street. She's lived there for several years now," Jim told me. "She sometimes comes into my shop – that's how I get the dolls to sell."

"What's her name? What's she like?" I asked.

"I'm not sure of her name," Jim replied. "It's something like 'Callamy'. She's a tall, red-haired woman. She owns many expensive coats. But she's got a hard-looking face and she doesn't say much when she comes in here. To tell you the truth, I'm glad when she goes." He stopped for a minute and then added, "I've never seen her smile."

I couldn't understand this. How could a woman like that make such a beautiful doll?

"I'll buy her," I said. Eleven pounds seemed a lot of money to pay for a doll. As I counted out the pound notes, I felt rather silly. Although the doll was a present for my niece, I knew the real reason why I had bought her – I couldn't leave her in that dusty window.

I took the doll home and there, in my small bedroom, she seemed to fill it with her loveliness. I carefully put her into a box which I then covered with brown paper. In the afternoon I went to the post office and posted it to my niece.

I thought that now I would forget about that doll – but I didn't. I couldn't stop thinking about it. How could that beautiful doll have been made by the woman Jim told me about?

Once I thought of trying to find out who she was, but many children were suddenly ill in the cold, wet weather and I was busy for several weeks. I forgot all about the woman – and the doll.

One day, a few weeks later, my telephone rang. A woman's voice said, "Is that Doctor Amony?"

"Yes," I said.

"Do you visit people who want to pay for treatment?" the woman asked.

"Yes, sometimes," I replied.

"How much does it cost?" she asked.

The voice sounded rather unpleasant. The woman seemed to care more about the money than the person who was ill. I replied, "A visit will cost five pounds – but if you really can't pay then I don't ask for the money."

"That's all right," she said. "I can pay five pounds. My name is Rose Callamit. The house where I live is next to the cake shop in Hardley Street. My rooms are on the second floor."

"I'll be there as soon as I can," I told her.

I arrived at the house ten minutes later. I went up the stairs. They were narrow, dusty and badly lit.

As I reached the top, the door opened and the unpleasant voice said, "Doctor Amony? Please come in. I'm Rose Callamit."

In front of me stood a tall woman with unnatural-looking, red hair. She had dark eyes and her lips were a bright, shiny red. She was between forty-five and fifty years old.

I was disappointed when I saw her, and my disappointment grew when I entered the front room. The furniture was cheaply made. On the cupboard in the corner were lots of small, glass bottles. There was no warmth here: it was a cold, ugly room.

And then behind the door I noticed the dolls. They were hanging from the walls and were thrown carelessly on the bed. They were all different but each of them had the same grace and loveliness that I had seen in the doll I had bought for my niece. It seemed impossible that this woman was the maker of these dolls.

"Aren't you too young to be a doctor?" Rose Callamit asked.

I answered her sharply because I was disappointed to find the dolls in this woman's home.

"I'm older than I look," I said, "but if you think I'm too young, I'll go," I finished, angrily.

She laughed at me. "There's no need to be angry, Doc!

You're very good-looking for a doctor."

"It's because I'm a doctor that I don't have time to waste. Are you the one who's ill?" I asked.

"No. It's my niece," she replied. "She's in the back room. I'll take you to her."

Before we went in, I had to know about the dolls. I asked, "Do you make these dolls?"

"Yes. Why?" she asked.

For some reason I felt very sad. "I bought one once for my niece," I said quietly.

She laughed. "I expect you paid a lot of money for it."

She led me through a hall to a smaller room at the back. As she started to open the door she shouted, "Mary, it's the doctor." Then as she pushed it wider to let me through, she said loudly, so that the girl could hear: "Don't be surprised when you see her, Doctor. Her left leg is twisted!"

The girl, Mary, was sitting in a chair by the window. As she heard these words, a look of deep misery came into her face. Again I was angry at this nasty woman. Her words were making Mary think about her leg.

Mary did not look more then twenty-five years old. But her face was very pale and her dark eyes seemed huge. It was as if her soul was dying. She was very ill.

From my first visit I was struck by the sweetness in her sad face. I remembered, too, her poor, thin body and her hair, which was dry and unhealthy. But I did see something that filled me with joy. She was surrounded by small tables. One of them was covered with paints and brushes. On the others were needles, thread and pieces of cloth of many different colours and sizes – all the things needed to make the dolls.

I could see that her illness was not caused by her

twisted leg. But it was her leg that caught my attention. It was the way she sat. If it was what I thought it was – it could be straightened with treatment.

"Can you walk, Mary?" I asked.

"Yes," she answered, quietly.

"Please walk to me," I asked, gently.

"Oh, don't," she said. "Don't make me."

I didn't want to make her suffer but I had to be sure. "I'm sorry, Mary," I said. "Please try."

She very carefully got up from her chair and limped towards me. I looked closely at her left leg. Yes, I was sure I was right.

"That's good," I said, and I smiled to show that I was pleased. I held out my hands to help her. As she looked up, I saw again the misery and hopelessness that she was feeling. She seemed to be crying out silently to me for help. Her hands lifted towards mine – and then they fell back to her sides. The hope was gone.

"How long have you been like this, Mary?" I asked.

Rose Callamit said, "Oh, Mary's had that twisted leg for almost ten years now. But I didn't ask you to come for that. She's ill. I want to know what's the matter with her."

Oh, yes, she was ill. She might even be dying. I knew that as soon as I saw her.

I expected Rose to leave the room, but she didn't. She laughed and said, "I'm staying here, Doctor Amony. You find out what's the matter with Mary and then you can tell me."

When I finished looking at Mary I went with Rose into the front room.

"Well?" she said.

"Did you know that her leg could be straightened?" I

asked. "With treatment she could be walking in——"

"That's enough!"

She shouted these words and it made me jump.

"Don't you dare say anything about that to her," she continued. "She's been looked at by people who know. I won't have some young fool raising her hopes. If you ever do, you won't come here again. I want to know what's the matter with her. She won't eat or sleep and she isn't working properly. What did you find out?"

"I don't know what's the matter with her yet," I replied, "but she's slowly being destroyed by something. I shall want to see her again, soon. I'm going to give her something to take. It should make her feel stronger. I'll call again in a few days."

"Don't you say anything about fixing her leg, you understand? If you do, I'll get another doctor," she added.

"All right," I said. I had to be able to visit Mary again. Perhaps when Mary was feeling better I might be able to talk about her leg. I would see ...

As I picked up my bag to leave I said, "I thought you said you made these dolls."

"I do," she said in an unpleasant way. "I draw them and I let Mary make them. It helps her to keep her mind off her leg; and the fact that she will never marry and have children."

As I walked out into the bright October sunshine I knew that Rose Callamit had lied. I had found out who was the sweet person who made those delightful dolls.

But happy though I was about this, I was very troubled about Mary. Unless I was able to find out what was wrong with her, I knew she would soon die.

During my next few visits I learned more about Mary. Her

name was Mary Nolan and when she was fifteen years old she had been in a car crash. Her mother and father had been killed and Mary was badly hurt. This crash was the cause of her twisted leg.

The court put Mary in the charge of Rose Callamit as there was no one else to look after her. Rose was willing to look after the young girl. She thought that Mary's father had been quite rich. When she found out that there was only a small amount of money she was unkind to Mary. She made her as unhappy as she could.

She never let Mary forget her leg. She seemed to be saying: "No man will love you. You will never get married and have children. No man would want a wife with a twisted leg."

As the years passed, Mary began to believe her aunt. So she stayed with her and did what her aunt wanted her to do. She had no reason to fight against her aunt and leave, so she lived a hopeless and unhappy life.

Then she started to make the dolls. Rose Callamit saw how lovely the dolls were and she knew they could be sold for lots of money. After she had sold a few, she made Mary work on them from morning until night.

This had continued for several years. But now Mary was ill. Although Rose did not have any love for Mary, she was clever enough to know that without Mary the money would end.

But I was still no nearer to finding out what was killing Mary. I could see that she was afraid of her aunt – but it wasn't that. And I couldn't find out from Mary herself, because her aunt was always with us. I felt that Mary found it difficult to say anything to me with Rose in the room.

I did not tell Mary that I thought I could mend her leg.

It was more important to discover why she didn't want to live any more.

For ten days Mary seemed to get better. I stopped her working on the dolls. I brought her some books to read and some chocolates to eat.

When I called the next time, she smiled at me for the first time since I had seen her.

"That's better!" I said, delighted. "You're to leave the dolls alone for another ten days. I want you to rest, sleep and read. Then we'll see."

But I could see that Rose was unhappy at these words.

When I called the next time she was waiting for me in her room. She said, "You don't need to come any more, Doctor Amony."

"But Mary ...?" I started to say.

"Mary is better now," she replied. "Goodbye, Doctor."

My eyes went to the box in the corner of the room. There were three new dolls lying on top of it. Their faces were as lovely as ever, but they seemed to me to have the look of death on them.

Suddenly I was frightened for Mary. I knew that Rose Callamit was lying. I wanted to push this woman aside and crash through the door and see Mary. But I was a doctor and when doctors are told to leave, it is their duty to go. I had not found out what was the matter with Mary and I supposed that Rose was asking another doctor to call.

So, sadly, I left. But in the days that followed I couldn't forget Mary. I was continually troubled about her.

Not long after this I became ill myself. It wasn't much at first, but as the days passed it could clearly be seen. I saw a doctor friend of mine, who said that he could find nothing wrong with my body. He said that I had, perhaps, been working too hard. But I knew that this wasn't the reason.

I continued to get worse. I didn't want to eat and I lost weight. I felt tired and restless. At night I didn't sleep properly. I sometimes dreamed that I saw Mary calling to me for help, while Rose Callamit was holding Mary in her ugly arms.

I began to look thin and pale. I couldn't forget that I had not been able to help her. She had wanted me to help her and I had done nothing.

One night I was so restless I couldn't sleep at all. I walked up and down my room thinking about myself and my illness. It seemed that I was suffering from the same illness as Mary. Suddenly I knew what the matter was: I was in love with Mary Nolan! It was because I couldn't see her and take care of her that I felt so ill and unhappy.

Now I knew why Mary was dying. She was dying because no one loved her and she had no one in the world to give her hope for the years to come. Her mother and father were dead. Her aunt just kept her for the money she got from selling the dolls. Mary had no friends and worst of all, because of her leg, she felt she was ugly. Her life was empty – except for the dolls.

I knew that I had to see her. I had to speak to her for a few minutes, alone – or she would be lost to me for ever.

That morning I telephoned Jim Carter at his shop. "This is Doctor Amony, Jim. Will you do me a favour?"

"Anything, Doc," Jim said. "After you saved my son's life last year, I'll do anything you ask."

"Thanks, Jim," I said. "Do you remember Mrs Rose Callamit, the doll woman? Well, the next time she comes into your shop, I want you to try and telephone me – then keep her talking. I need twenty minutes. All right? Good. I'll bless you for the rest of my life."

I was frightened that he would telephone while I was out. So, each evening I put my head round the door of his shop. But he just shook his head to show me that there was no news.

Then one day at five o'clock in the afternoon the telephone rang. It was Jim. He just said, "You could go now."

It only took me two or three minutes to run to the house where Mary lived. When I got there I ran up the stairs. I hoped I would be able to get in. Luckily, the door was not locked. Rose had only expected to be gone for a few minutes.

I hurried into Mary's room. She looked so thin now and very ill. She still had the paints and pieces of cloth around her. It was as if she wanted to make one more doll before she died.

She looked up when I came in. Her eyes opened wide in surprise when she saw me. She thought it would be Rose. She said my name; not "Doctor Amony" but "Stephen".

"Mary!" I cried. "Thank God I'm in time. I've come to help you. I know what's been making you ill."

"Does it matter now?" she whispered.

"There's still time, Mary," I said. "I know your secret. I know how to make you well. But you must listen while I tell you."

She just closed her eyes and said, quietly, "No. Don't, *please*. Let me go. I don't want to know. It will be over soon."

I sat down and held her hand. "Mary, please listen," I asked, gently. "Each person has a certain store of love to give out through their life. This store is built up when they are children. They receive the love from their family as they grow up.

"As they grow older, the love is given out and the store has to be refilled by kindness, happiness, joy and hope. That way there is always something left. But your store of love has been emptied, Mary, until there is nothing left."

I was not sure that she could still hear me, but I wanted her to live so much. I had to go on.

"It was your aunt," I said. "She took away all your hopes for love and happiness. And later on," I continued, "she did a far worse thing – she took away your children." I almost whispered these last words – but I felt I had to say them.

I looked at Mary. Had I killed her? I, who loved her so much? Then I felt her small hand move in mine and her eyes slowly opened. She seemed almost glad I had said these words. This gave me hope so I continued to try and make her understand.

"Oh, yes. Those dolls were your children, Mary. When you thought you had lost your chance to love and be a mother, you made those enchanted dolls. Into each one you put some of your love. You made them with gentleness and care, and you loved them as if they were your own children.

"Then each one was taken away and you were given nothing in return. You continued to use up your store of love until even your soul was drawn from you. People can die when they have no love left inside them."

As I finished speaking she moved. She seemed to understand what I was saying.

"But you won't die, Mary," I cried, "because *I* love you! Do you hear me? I love you and I cannot live without you."

"Love me?" she whispered. "But I have a twisted leg. How can you love me?"

"That doesn't matter to me, Mary. I still love you," I said, gently. "But Rose lied to you. Your leg can be straightened. In a year you'll be walking like any other girl."

Then, as I continued to look at her, I saw tears of joy in her eyes. She smiled at me in complete trust and put her arms out to me.

I gathered her up in my arms. She weighed so little – she was like a bird. She held on to me as I put my coat round her to keep her warm. Then I carried her across the room.

Suddenly we heard the front door shut and the sound of running footsteps. Then Mary's door crashed open as Rose Callamit came into the room, angrily. I felt Mary start to shake with fear. She hid her face in my neck.

But Rose was too late. There was nothing she could do now, and she knew it. Not a word was spoken as I walked past her, holding Mary close to me. I went out of her front door, down the stairs and into the street.

Outside, the sun shone on the dusty street and the children were playing noisily as I carried Mary home.

That was three years ago. As I write this, Mary is playing with our son. Our second child will be born in a few weeks.

She doesn't make the dolls now. She doesn't need to. But I silently bless the day when I first saw, and fell in love with, the enchanted doll in Jim Carter's shop window.

The Silver Swans

My name is Doctor Horatio Fundoby – but I am not a doctor who treats people when they are ill. I am called a doctor because I have spent many, many years studying. The subject that I studied was history, and I am now one of the people in charge of the British Museum, in London.

Every Sunday afternoon I walk along a path, in Chelsea, on the bank of the River Thames. A lot of artists live in Chelsea, and people often think that *I* am an artist because of the way I dress and look. I have a white beard, I carry a black wooden stick, and I wear a large, old hat. I have had the hat for more than forty years and I always wear it for my walks.

I enjoy my walks very much. There is so much to see and hear. There are the seagulls, that cry noisily as they fly over the river, and there are the many boats which pass.

Along this bank of the river there are several old houseboats tied up. People buy these houseboats because they like living on the water, and they enjoy the sights and sounds of a busy river. They paint the boats in bright colours and they look very colourful.

One Sunday afternoon I was standing by the houseboats, looking across the river. In the deepest water in the middle of the Thames I could see a beautiful, white sailing ship. It was called the *Poseidon*. The back of the ship was rather unusual and as soon as I saw it I knew that the ship was owned by Lord Struve. He was a great underwater diver and a scientist of ocean life. Near to the *Poseidon* was a large ship from South America and a dirty Spanish boat, which carried goods to Britain.

Then I noticed one of the houseboats near the bank. It was called the *Nerine* and it was very colourful. Although the boat was grey, parts of it were painted in bright colours: the chimney was yellow, the door was blue and the large wooden cover at the front of the boat was painted bright red. There were some steps leading from the boat to the bank of the river – these were painted blue, like the door.

As I was looking at the boat I saw a young girl pushing back the cover – at least she was trying to. She wanted to get out through the cover, but I could see that she was stuck halfway out of the hole. Just then she saw me. She didn't shout at me but her lips formed the words: "I'm stuck!"

I hurried towards the *Nerine*. I had to walk down the blue wooden steps, as the *Nerine* was sitting on the bottom of the river: the water of the Thames lay several feet away.

I went carefully along the deck of the boat until I reached the girl. The red paint had dried and the cover wouldn't open any further. I used my stick to free it and a few moments later the girl climbed out on to the deck.

She was about twenty years old. She was wearing old, blue trousers – which were covered in paint – and a grey shirt. I thought she looked rather beautiful.

She looked at me with big, green eyes – they were the loveliest part of her face.

"You *are* a dear man," she said. "Do you know who you make me think of? You're just like——"

"The old gentlemen you see in the British Museum," I finished for her.

"Oh, I'm sorry. That was bad manners," she said, smiling gently.

"But I am an old gentleman," I said. "Please don't think any more about it. In fact I do work at the British Museum. I'm Doctor Horatio Fundoby."

"Oh!" she said. "The British Museum!" She was silent for a moment, and then she asked, "Would you like to see my octopus?"

"I'd be delighted," I said, smiling.

She led me down through the blue door into a cool, green room. The curtains were drawn but some light came through the cloth. I could see a small bed, bookshelves and paintings. Then I noticed two glass containers: one large and one small. In the small container were two seahorses and in the large one was the octopus.

She was staring at it. "Isn't it beautiful?" she said. "Sometimes I sit and look at it for hours."

"Does it have a name?" I asked.

"Oh, I just call it Octopus," she replied.

"And you? What's your name?" I continued.

After a moment she said, "My name is Thetis."

"Ah," I said, "that's the name of one of the water people in the Greek stories of long ago. Thetis was the daughter of Nereus and Doris, who lived at the bottom of the sea."

She pulled her lip, thoughtfully. "My real name is Alice," she said. "I call myself Thetis because I'd like to live at the bottom of the ocean."

As she said this, I could understand the reason for her cool, green room. Being in her room was like being under water. It was rather dark – the only lights being the ones that lit the glass containers. The paintings on the wall were in blues and greens and showed fish and other underwater animals. I was certain that she was the artist. She looked as if she could almost be a water-fairy herself, with her small nose, huge eyes and pretty, short, brown hair.

"Would you like me to sing for you?" she asked.

"Oh, please do," I replied, delighted.

She reached behind a curtain and pulled out a beautiful guitar. She sat down, closed her eyes and played some notes on the guitar. They filled the room with a lovely sound.

"My song is called *The silver swans*," she said. Then she sang in a sweet, gentle voice:

> *How shall I know my true love?*
> *When will my true heart speak to me?*
> *O when the silver swans come sailing,*
> *Then I will know my true love,*
> *Then I will be with my true love,*
> *For ever with my true love.*

It was a beautiful song but I felt that there was a sadness behind the words. The words showed wisdom and under-standing – but I knew that the young girl in front of me knew nothing about being in love.

"That was lovely," I said. "Who wrote it?"

Thetis opened her eyes. "I did. It's mine."

"Do you often write songs?" I asked, surprised.

"Only when they come into my head," she replied.

Suddenly she moved to the edge of her seat.

"How *will* I know my true love?" she asked, seriously. "How will I know when I'm really in love?"

"How old are you, Thetis? Have you ever been in love?" I asked.

"I'm twenty-one," she replied, "and no, I don't think I've ever been in love." She stopped for a moment and then she continued: "How will I know? Who will tell me when I am? You're so old and wise. Can't you help me?"

She looked pale and unhappy, so I thought carefully before I answered her questions.

At last I replied, "When he is ill and 'unbeautiful' and you can still love him – then you can be sure."

"When he is ill and 'unbeautiful'. . ." she said to herself, quietly.

She sat there thinking. Then suddenly she remembered I was there. "Oh, I'm sorry, I'm forgetting my manners," she said. "Would you like some tea, Doctor Fundoby?"

"That would be lovely. Thank you," I replied.

She disappeared for several minutes, leaving me to look round the room again.

At last she returned, carrying the tea things. She poured out the tea. As she raised her cup to her lips, she said again, "When he is ill and 'unbeautiful'. Oh, thank you, Doctor Fundoby!" She smiled at me.

We talked for about half an hour. She told me about her mother and father, who also lived in London. But she told me that she wanted to live by herself on this houseboat – because it was on the water, which she loved. She told me that she had a job which she did in the evenings, but she did not tell me what it was.

Suddenly I began to feel rather unwell. But before I could decide what was the matter with me, Thetis asked if I would like to go out on deck.

There was not much room at the back of the boat – but it was just wide enough for the two of us. Then I saw with surprise that the boat was now surrounded by water.

As we stood there four dirty white swans went past us. Their feathers were covered in oil, coal dust and dirt from the river, and their eyes looked very unfriendly.

As Thetis looked at them, I said, smiling, "Perhaps they're the silver swans in your song. Perhaps you're going to meet your true love."

She only said: "These swans are a dirty grey silver."

At that moment a small wooden boat came up to us. There was a tall, well-built man in the boat – he looked about thirty-five years old. He was wearing a blue sailing top and dark blue trousers. He had wavy, black hair, a beard, and bright, blue eyes.

"Hello there!" he shouted, his white teeth shining against his dark beard. "Have you a needle and thread I could use to mend my trousers? I caught them on a piece of wood."

"Certainly," Thetis called back. "If you climb up here I'll mend them for you."

The sailor laughed. "I think I ought to do it," he said, "because of where they've been caught!"

"Oh, I understand!" Thetis said, smiling. Then she went to find the needle and thread.

When she returned she put them carefully in a piece of cloth and threw them into the boat.

The sailor caught them. "Clever child," he said. "Thanks very much. I won't be long." He let the boat go back some way and then tied it up next to another boat.

We stood watching as he sat there with his back towards us, mending his trousers. As we stood there several waves from a large boat, which was passing, made the *Nerine* go up and down. I suddenly felt very sick.

Thetis turned to say something but stopped when she saw my face. "Oh, you poor man!" she cried. "I'd forgotten that the movement of boats sometimes makes people ill. Come with me – I've got a bottle of something

44

which will soon make you feel better."

She helped me down into the cool, green room and made me sit in a chair. I was feeling very ill indeed. She went to a small cupboard and got a small brown bottle from it. She poured out some of the liquid into a spoon and gave it to me.

"They discovered this stuff during the Second World War," she said. "Some of the sailors used to suffer badly from the movement of ships on the water. You'll feel fine in a few minutes. Just sit there quietly." She went out on deck.

I heard her shout to the man in the boat: "Hello there! What's your name?"

"Hadley. Richard Hadley," he called back. "What's yours?"

I knew I had heard that name before – but I couldn't remember where.

"Thetis," she replied.

There was silence for a minute, then he said, "Oh, that's the name of the daughter of Nereus and Doris in the Greek stories of long ago. They lived at the bottom of the sea." He was silent again. Then I heard him call: "Where's your father?"

"He isn't my father," Thetis said. "He's an old gentleman who's visiting me. He's feeling rather sick so I've given him something to take."

I heard the laugh in the sailor's voice as he shouted, "What! Sick! – on that old, flat-bottomed boat? Why, being on there is almost the same as being on dry land."

Another boat passed and the *Nerine* suddenly moved up and down again. But, thank God, the liquid was beginning to work.

"It isn't an old boat," Thetis said, seriously, "it's my home. And it does move up and down a great deal sometimes. You need a strong stomach."

"Oh yes, I'm sure you do," he said. But I knew from the way he said it that he didn't really believe her.

"Really, it's true," she continued. "You might get sick yourself, one day."

The sailor laughed loudly. "Who, me? Listen, child. I've sailed every ocean and sea there is and in all kinds of weather – and I haven't been sick yet."

I heard Thetis say, "There's always a first time. Would you like to try?"

"Let me know when it gets really rough," he said.

I heard his boat touch against the *Nerine*, as he added: "You're not as young as I thought you were. I'm sorry I called you child. Perhaps I'll try out your boat sometime. Well, thanks again for the needle and thread."

At last I began to feel better. When I went up on deck Thetis was standing looking out across the river. She was watching the sailor as he went out towards the lovely, white ship.

"Oh," she said, "you're better. Good. That stuff always works." Then she added, "He said some very unkind things, didn't he?"

I started to say, "We-e-e-ll," when she continued, dreamily, "But wasn't he beautiful?"

I did not see my friend for several weeks. Then, on a rainy Sunday, as I walked past the houseboats, I heard my name being called.

"Doctor Fundoby! Doctor Fundoby!"

I turned round and saw Thetis running up the steps from the *Nerine*. She ran up to me and said, "Doctor

46

Fundoby! What shall I do? My octopus has eaten off one of his arms."

I replied, "They often do when people keep them, even though they feed them very well."

"Oh well," she said. "Thanks for telling me that – it makes me feel a lot better."

She turned and went back to her boat. As she reached the deck I called out to her, "Did your sailor ever come back?"

"Yes," she answered, and disappeared into the boat.

A few days later a friend asked me to go and see a play called *The Unwanted*, at Wyndham's Theatre in London. People said that the young actress, Alice Adams, was very good.

"One day," my friend said, "she'll be a great actress."

When the play started I couldn't believe my eyes. The young actress was Thetis! I remembered, then, that she had told me that her real name was Alice. So this was her evening job!

It was a sad play. Thetis played a young girl who falls in love with an older man. In the end he leaves her and in her misery she kills herself. Thetis played the part with such deep feeling and understanding that she made me believe she was that poor girl – and I wept for her at the end of the play.

The next Sunday I visited her on her boat. There was now another glass container in her room. There were two large fish in it. She had been sitting in front of it, watching them. She gave me some of the liquid from the brown bottle – and I drank it even though the boat was not moving much.

"My dear," I said. "Why didn't you tell me who you

were? I was at Wyndham's last week."

"I did tell you," she said. "But this is who I am *here*. It's who I really want to be."

"You played the part so well. I cried at the end," I added, quietly. "How can you put so much feeling into the part night after night? How can you show all that pain and unhappiness when you say you have never been in love?"

"Oh," she replied, thinking for a moment, "that's the other side of me. I just do it."

She saw me looking at the glass container. "He gave them to me," she said.

"The sailor? Where did he get them?" I asked.

"From the bottom of the river."

"Indeed! How?" I asked.

"He said he went down and looked for them," she replied.

Now I remembered who Richard Hadley was – and I wondered whether she knew.

And I wondered whether she was to be heart-broken, like the girl in the play.

"Is he in love with you?" I asked.

"He laughs at me and says unkind things," she said. "Does that mean he is?"

"And you?" I asked. "Are you in love with him?"

"I don't know," she cried. "I don't know! I don't know! Oh, Doctor Fundoby, how I hate being young!"

She put her head on my shoulder and started to cry – while I tried to say something that would make her feel better.

The following Sunday I went for my usual walk. It was very windy. The river was rough and when I saw the *Nerine* she was rolling badly from side to side. Thinking of Thetis, I hurried towards the boat. Her room was small and the glass containers could be dangerous if they fell.

I noticed that the blue door was open, so I quickly went down the steps. As I reached the last step I heard a deep cry from Thetis's room. I was afraid that something had happened to her so I hurried in.

There, a completely unexpected sight met my eyes. Lying on the small bed was a very sick Richard Hadley. Thetis was sitting on the edge of the bed holding his head in one of her arms. His skin was a sickly grey colour. His face was pale and his hair was sticky and in knots. At first I thought he was dying – then the boat moved suddenly and I understood why he was like this.

"Thetis!" I cried. "The liquid! Quickly! Where is it?"

"Oh-h-h!" cried the unhappy man. "Won't you all go away and let me die in peace!"

"I love him!" Thetis said, joyfully holding his poor head in her arms. "Oh, now I know that I love him. He *is* very ill, isn't he, Doctor Fundoby? And I love him even more than when he's well."

I went to the cupboard where Thetis kept the brown bottle of liquid. It was locked. I looked at Thetis. She looked sorry but said, "He won't say that he'll marry me." Then she added, looking down at him: "I don't mind being a poor sailor's wife. When you sail away – I'll come with you and we can sail round the world together. I'll even sleep in a hammock."

I had to stop myself laughing at her words: Thetis had no idea of what a sailor's life was really like, or who Richard Hadley was.

The miserable man, who was too weak to get up, cried out: "All right, all right, I'll marry you! I'll do anything you like, if you'll just go away and let me die."

I was beginning to feel very ill myself, so I cried, "Thetis! You hard-hearted girl! Give me the key at once. How can you make him suffer – the man you say you love?"

She untied a piece of blue silk from around her neck – the key was on it. She kept her eyes looking down as she handed me the key, and I knew that she was sorry for what she had done.

As I opened the cupboard, I heard her say, quietly, "He's sailed on every ocean and sea in all kinds of weather."

After taking some of the liquid myself, I gave some to the great underwater diver and scientist – Richard Hadley, Lord Struve.

Thetis looked at me. "Will you come and see us get married, Doctor Fundoby?" she asked.

I was still feeling sick, and I was disappointed with the way she had behaved, so I replied, "If he marries you after what you've made him suffer, I shall be sure he's mad."

Lord Struve must have suddenly felt better because he sat up and said, "I'm glad to hear you say that, Doctor Fundoby. Promises made in these conditions shouldn't mean anything."

"But it was you who wanted to come on to the Nerine in this weather. I did warn you," she said, sadly.

"I came," he said, the colour returning to his face, "because I wanted to tell you that I love you."

"Well then," Thetis asked, simply, "why didn't you?"

He looked for a minute as though he didn't know what to say. Then he said, suddenly, "Because I felt ill. Now listen, Thetis. If you're going to marry me you'd better know who I am and what I do."

"I don't care who you are or what you do," Thetis

replied. "I love you."

I was feeling better, so I said, "And your acting?"

Lord Struve looked at me in surprise. "Whose acting?" he asked.

"Good heavens!" I cried. "Are you *both* blind? This is Alice Adams who's been in the play *The Unwanted* at Wyndham's for the last two years."

He stared. "This child? She is a child, isn't she?"

Thetis nodded her head. But I said: "She's England's best young actress and she's twenty-one."

He stood up. "Yes!" he cried. "I remember reading something a long time ago. I've just come back from the Galapagos," he continued, "and I haven't heard anything about England for nearly two years."

Thetis jumped up and ran over to him. "Oh, please," she asked, in an excited voice, "take me there. All my life I've wanted to go to the Galapagos. Are sailors allowed to take their wives with them when they go?"

Lord Struve cried, "Heavens, Thetis! I'm not a sailor. I'm a——" He stopped. He seemed to find it difficult to say: "I'm a lord." He finished by saying "a sort of undersea diver. I do things under water. But your acting——"

Before he could finish, Thetis said: "It doesn't matter. I never wanted to be an actress. When I went for the job they said I could be good, one day. I only do it to get money to buy myself guitars and octopuses, and the *Nerine*. Do you know what a good octopus costs?"

Lord Struve held both her arms. "Thetis, can you be serious for a minute? Do you really mean you'd give all that up for me and come away?"

"Of course," she replied. "What I really want, more than anything in the world, is to walk with you on the bottom of the ocean near the Galapagos, now that ..." She stopped for a moment, thinking. "Now that, thanks to Doctor Fundoby, I'm sure I love you."

For another minute Lord Struve held her two arms while he looked up to heaven with a very happy look on his face. It was as if he couldn't quite believe what he had heard. He said something very quietly – it sounded like a prayer of thanks.

Then he held Thetis close to him and looked over her head at me. "You know, Doctor Fundoby," he said, softly, "God is sometimes too wonderful to understand – the way He has answered one man's prayer."

And so the song of *The silver swans* came true. Thetis, the water-fairy married her god of the sea – Richard Hadley.

I still walk along by the River Thames, but I don't enjoy the walk as much as I used to.

Lady Struve, her husband, guitar and octopus have gone off to some beautiful island in the Pacific Ocean. There, they dive and work together among the wonderful undersea plants and animals.

A family have bought the *Nerine* and painted her a dark brown colour. They've changed the name to the *Nelson*, which is the name of one of the greatest officers in the British Navy – Sir Horatio Nelson. If he was alive now I don't think he'd be very pleased to see the boat that is named after him.

As I pass her every Sunday I see a line stretching from the back of the boat to the front. It is filled with washing – mostly little children's clothes. And I wonder, as I pass, whether they too have strong stomachs like Thetis – or whether she gave them the name of that powerful liquid in the brown bottle.

Questions

Questions on each story

The Snow Goose
1   Why did the people of Chelmbury stare at Philip?
    (Because . . .)
2   What had he built an enclosure for? (For . . .)
3   What did the girl bring to Philip?
4   Where did she find it?
5   What country did the snow goose come from?
6   What name did Philip give to the snow goose?
7   Where did Fritha live?
8   When did the snow goose return to the enclosure?
9   Which season did the snow goose spend away from the
    lighthouse?
10 One year the snow goose didn't go away. Which year was
    that?
11 What did Philip put into his boat?
12 Where was he preparing to go?
13 Where were the soldiers?
14 Why couldn't Fritha go with Philip? (Because . . .)
15 Who did Private Potton tell his story to?
16 What was the name of Private Potton's friend?
17 Which ship brought Private Potton across the Channel?
18 Who did Private Potton mean by "'Im"?
19 How many men did the boat take at a time?
20 Where was the snow goose?
21 When Private Potton was on the *Kentish Maid,* where did the
    man in the boat go?
22 Who tells the second part of the story?
23 What happened to the sailing boat?
24 Where was Fritha when the snow goose flew over?
25 What happened to the lighthouse and the enclosure?

The Enchanted Doll
 1 What is Stephen Amony's work?
 2 What was unusual about the doll's clothes and face?
 3 How much did Stephen pay for the doll?
 4 Who telephoned, and what did she ask?
 5 Who made the dolls?
 6 What was the matter with her leg?
 7 How was Mary's leg hurt?
 8 Why couldn't Stephen find out what was killing Mary?
   (Because . . .)
 9 What was Stephen himself suffering from?
10 What did he ask Jim Carter to do?
11 When Jim rang, where did Stephen go?
12 What did Mary call him?
13 When (in Stephen's belief) is each person's store of love built
   up?
14 How is the store of love refilled?
15 What were Mary's "children"?
16 What did Mary put into each of the dolls?
17 Why did Mary think Stephen couldn't love her?
   (Because she had . . .)
18 What happened after Stephen picked Mary up?
19 Where did Stephen take Mary?
20 What happened to Mary in the end?

The Silver Swans
 1 What is Dr Fundoby's special subject?
 2 When does he walk along the river bank?
 3 Who owned the *Poseidon*?
 4 Where was the girl stuck?
 5 What did the girl offer to show Dr Fundoby?
 6 Who was Thetis in the ancient Greek stories?
 7 Who wrote the song?
 8 When (according to Dr Fundoby) can Thetis know she is in
   love?
 9 What did the man want a needle and thread for? (To . . .)
10 What made Dr Fundoby feel sick?
11 What did Thetis do about his sickness?
12 "There's always a first time." What did Thetis mean?
13 What had the octopus done?

14 What play was Thetis acting in?
15 Who gave her the two fish?
16 What was the matter with Richard Hadley the following week?
17 Why did Dr Fundoby call Thetis "hard-hearted"?
18 Who was Richard Hadley?
19 Where did Thetis want to walk with him?
20 Where did Lord and Lady Struve go?

Questions on the whole book

These are harder questions. Read the Introduction, and think hard about the questions before you answer them. Some of them ask for your opinion, and there is no fixed answer.

The Snow Goose
 1 Why did Philip Rhayader live alone?

 2 What were his main interests?

 3 *a* Why was he not in one of the fighting forces in the war of 1939–1945?
   b What do these words tell you about him: "At last I can do something to help in this war"?
   c Fritha called to the snow goose: "Take care of him, Princess." Do you think the snow goose did try to take care of Philip? How?

 4 *a* When did Fritha realise that Philip loved her?
   b When did she realise that she loved Philip?

The Enchanted Doll
 5 What was so unusual about the doll in the shop window?

 6 Why do you think Mary made the dolls so beautiful?

 7 At the end of the story, why doesn't Mary need to make dolls?

 8 At the end, Stephen says, "I silently bless the day when I first saw ... the enchanted doll in Jim Carter's window."
   a Why does he bless that day?
   b Why "silently"?
   c What does he mean by "enchanted"?

The Silver Swans
 9 Where do the words "silver swans" first come into the story?

10 What do you suppose Lord Struve had been doing in the Galapagos Islands?

11 Was Thetis really "hard-hearted"? Can you explain your answer?

12 Which of the three stories do you like best? Why?

New words

clip
    cut the feathers of a bird's
    wing

disappointment
    unhappiness because
    something you hoped for
    has not happened

doll
    a child's plaything in the
    form of a very small person,
    especially a baby

dot
    a small point like this →·

enchanted
    made different by magic

fiction
    stories about things that
    didn't really happen

hammock
    a hanging bed. Ordinary
    sailors (not officers) used to
    sleep in them.

hunchback
    (a person with) a badly bent
    back

lighthouse
    a tower with a light to guide
    ships or to warn them of
    danger

limp
    walk with uneven steps

lonely
    away from people; unhappy
    because alone

marsh, marshland
    land that is always wet

mine
    a metal container which will
    explode if a ship touches it

novel
    a long story with invented
    people and happenings,
    printed as a book

octopus
    a deep-sea creature with
    eight arms round its mouth

private
    an ordinary soldier, not an
    officer (or sergeant, etc)

seahorse
    a very small fish with a neck
    and head that look like those
    of a horse

swan
    a bird with a long neck,
    found on rivers and lakes

thread
    a line of cotton, wool, silk,
    etc, used in sewing

wild-fowler
    a person who shoots wild
    birds